Before the Farmhouse Burned Down

Holly Riordan

THOUGHT
CATALOG
Books

This book was designed by KJ Parish and published by Thought Catalog Books, a publishing house owned by The Thought & Expression Company. It was printed in 2018.

ISBN 978-1-945796-95-1

MARY

JULY 12, 1963

Yesterday marked my thirteenth birthday. My sister helped clear room in the barn so the kids from school could sit on hay bales and tap their toes to the radio while I glided through the crowd in an oversized pink dress that covered the markings dug deep into my back. Twelve of them scabbed over with time and one was fresh, raised, red, and raw.

As my sister loaded the horses into their stables that morning, I heard my parents making their own preparations. Their footsteps scraped across the hall planks, and my body tensed like the wood had been pried up and shoved beneath my fingernails.

They slithered into my bedroom, hovered above my mattress, and waited for me to flip onto my stomach. I obeyed their silent instructions and the warmth of fingers wrapped around my shoulder, making the blade tip feel even colder. When it dug into my pale back and split the flesh, I shoved my knuckles into my mouth to keep from screaming and curled my toes to keep from kicking. After my veins were drained into a mason jar swishing with thirteen years of blood, I scrambled to find an old shirt to stop the flow and cotton to tape the wound.

The rest of the day, even when my friends grabbed my hand to twirl me in dance and snuck liquor into the apple juice cupped in my palm, I was distracted by my heartbeat thumping hard inside of my wound like it was trying to escape and wiggle far, far away from the farmhouse.

CHAPTER I

My grandmother swipes a brush as thin as a cat claw across her canvas while I sip from my third glass of wine, smudging baby-blue paint across the stem.

Last birthday, I baked her homemade cupcakes topped with chunks of strawberry and served them on a decorative platter—a plate with a hand-sketched maple tree and the names of her seven children dangling from each branch. Her guests gobbled the cupcakes before she took a single bite and she stored the plate in a cupboard to keep it safe because she deemed it *too pretty to ruin*. A complete waste of effort on my end.

This year, I decided to give her an experience in place of a present: one-on-one bonding time with her favorite granddaughter. A night where we could drink house wine and gossip about her cranky neighbor across the road and create artwork to hang on her wall instead of shoving it deep in a drawer somewhere.

"Honeybee," she says, dipping her bristles in water before switching colors, "do you think I'll get in trouble if I do something different?"

I tip my head, glancing at the instructor weaving through the labyrinth of paint-splattered tables. He gives step-by-step instructions on how to mimic the example painting in front of the room, a white beach house on the edge of sun-tinted water.

"You've always been a rule breaker. Why stop now?" I say, then give her a soft nudge. "Hey, I'll do my own thing, too. That way, he can yell at me if he wants. I can take him, don't you think?"

She swats away the invisible bicep I flex and laughs, a low tinkle against my ears.

I push my lips into a smile because we used to have to tell her to quiet down, *stop laughing so hard, stop singing so loud, stop stomping your feet so hard*. Now, she sings in hums and taps her cane on the floor to music, but sometimes she fails to get the rhythm right.

When the instructor squirts a glob of white onto a paper plate to shade the house we've drawn, my grandmother picks up blue. She paints the whole structure the same shade, from the pillars to the roof, and I realize it looks like the childhood house in her old photographs. Her farmhouse.

She explained the strange color scheme when I first found her scrapbook, empty aside from a few slots filled with Polaroids of the farm and its animals. As a kid, everyone else ignored my never-ending questions. They told me to ask a teacher or a preacher to wiggle out of an awkward conversation, but my grandmother gave the uncensored answers. To almost everything.

"Do you stick pins in your voodoo dolls to curse people?" I asked once, my legs dangling off the edge of her bed, arms reaching toward the skinny sticks wrapped in yellow yarn.

"No, I whisper wishes into them and they act as good luck. They can bring love, health, prosperity. Not revenge. Never revenge."

"What about the horseshoe hanging over the doorway; why is it facing up like that?"

"If you hang it the other way 'round, the luck will fall out."

"And the farmhouse? Why are all your pictures of it blue? Shouldn't it be red like in storybooks?"

"People used to seal their barns with linseed oil and the rust would turn it red. No other reason for that color. Blue is fine as any."

She spoke to me like an adult before I hit puberty, treating me as a true equal, a teammate, a trusted friend.

I try to do the same now, even when an accident prompts me to wash her sheets. Even when I struggle to heave her wheelchair up the porch steps. Even when her memory slips and she calls me by the wrong name, Margaret or Mary or May.

But now, the gears in her mind are making up for past mistakes because her hands stay steady, her lines pin straight. The image she creates matches the photograph in my memory, every window inserted on the right wall and every fencepost in place. She even adds a piglet on the lawn with a little more red than white, making it look smeared in blood rather than covered in pink.

I wonder if her spotted hands could draw her current house that well, the one she moved into fifty years ago with four children and a husband about to be killed by a heart attack. Sometimes she asks where we are when we're sitting on the edge of her mattress, watching the crows flitter to the feeder outside her window. Sometimes she forgets how much the place means to her, to all of us. She never forgets the farmhouse, though.

When the class ends, the instructor circles the room one last time to look at our finished work. Mine is far off from the example landscape, the wine weighing my fingers to lead, leaving streaks across the page I am too lazy to fix.

The instructor gives me a *that-came-out-nice* with unsmiling eyes but pauses above my grandmother, saying, "Look at this. This is beautiful. This is magic. Would you believe some people mess up when they follow me step-by-step? And trust me, the lesson is idiot-proof. But you created this on your own. You could teach the class next time."

He gives her a wink and my grandmother smiles close-lipped, too embarrassed to reveal her missing teeth. Back before her gums and flesh and nails turned yellow, she would have given him the finger. She would have called him a womanizer. She would have made jokes about how he should keep his hands to himself, regardless of their age difference.

"Come on, grandma," I say, shoving back the memories and helping her onto moccasined feet. "It's time to go home."

†

Our driver drops us off in a pebbled driveway at Chestnut Street. The two-story house contains a blackened lawn where the cousins used to play kickball and an old oak tree tilts toward the roof, one lightning bolt away from ripping a hole through the shingles. From the moment my feet crunch against grass, I see the shadow of my uncle pacing back and forth through the living-room windows.

"You're back so late I thought Slender Man ate you," he says when he steps outside, sipping from his energy drink.

I steal the can, check the calorie count. "This stuff is bad for your blood pressure. Also, Slender Man doesn't eat people. You should know this."

"I could use a slender man," grandma says without seeing the humor.

Before I have the chance to tease her, my uncle takes ahold of her arm and leads her up the porch steps. "She shouldn't have been on her feet all day," he says. "You should have taken her wheelchair."

"It's good for her to stretch her muscles. We weren't out long. And she had her cane. I'm not a monster." I lift the lime-green can like I'm giving a toast. "Get it…?"

"She could have fell. She could have busted her head open or broken a hip."

He continues to list off the injuries she could have acquired during the evening and I resist an eye roll. I remind myself he complains because he worries. He worries because he cares.

Unlike the rest of the family, who refuse to drop by to change her bedpan and also refuse to shell out the money for a retirement home, my uncle sticks by her side. Seven children, twelve grandchildren, and he does the work for all of them. With my help on weekends.

Once my grandmother gets settled inside the dining room out of earshot from the kitchen my uncle ushers me into, he asks how the night went. I brag about how she looked more alert than she has in weeks, months even. He ruins the mood by mentioning how the ladies at work told him that happens right before the end. Their energy spikes and then drops down to a flat line. With that, he grabs an Ensure from the fridge, leaves it on the table for her with a bended straw, and retires to the couch. He sleeps there now, closer to her bed, so he can hear her stir in the night.

I push his pessimism from my mind and search for empty space to hang the painting. The sea-green wallpaper in the dining room is cluttered with dreamcatchers and flea-market artwork. The only leftover space is situated beside the swinging door separating the kitchen. I ask my grandmother if she minds me sticking a nail through the wood, but instead of giving an answer, she waves me over to the table to join her.

"Did you have fun today?" I ask, moving the dirty pile of laundry from the seat cushion to the carpet. A few stray sweatshirts remain draped across the back, but I lean against them.

"Oh. So much, honeybee." She cups my sweat-slick hand with an icy one. "I want you to take mine. My farmhouse."

"And leave my crappy beach scene on your wall? No way. Yours is beautiful. You deserve to look at pretty things—and since I can't be here all the time, that painting will have to do."

She bows her head, letting the bangs from her wig drape over her bad eye, the one with the scar. "I keep certain things in this house to remind me where I came from. I want this picture to do that for you. I want it to remind you how good you have it. Compared to my childhood. To what happened."

I squeeze her palm to stop the words like a clamp to the mouth. Stress could make her health problems worse. It could activate her asthma, her arthritis.

In her healthier days, I begged her to tell stories about her past. The style of car she drove. The type of clothing she wore. Her first crush. Her first boyfriend. I wanted in-depth details, bombing her with questions she left unanswered. Even in elementary school, when my class filled out family trees for a history project, she refused to give me a list of names. The secrets only made me thirstier for the truth.

She never spoke a word to the rest of the family, either, but we concocted a story we agreed on. As a little girl, the foster home snatched her away. Separated her from her siblings. As far as her birth parents were concerned, we made dark assumptions. Alcoholic. Addict. Abuser. We decided she never spoke about her younger years because it brought too much pain.

"What do you say, honeybee?" my grandmother asks, squeezing my hand back like a faint heartbeat.

"I would be honored to have your painting. I'll put it right above my headboard so all the boys who come and go can admire it."

"Good," she says. "A lot of people will see it then."

I hear my uncle's firecracker laugh from the other room.

"Are you serious? Do you honestly think they'll be looking at your painting when they could be drooling over this toned, tanned body?" I say, striking a pose with my pale, flabby arms.

She swats my hand back into place, a smile tugging at her

chapped lips. We spend a few minutes sharing silence in the cove of her living room before I rummage for nails to hang my poor impression of a beach house on her wall.

"From far away, it almost looks like a Picasso," I say after my work is done.

"Almost."

She lets me kiss her forehead. Lets me shepherd her into bed. Lets me cocoon her in the covers. When I hear the ragged sound of her snoring, I give myself permission to leave with her farmhouse clutched to my chest, close to my cracking heart.

CHAPTER II

MARY

JULY 9, 1966

Felix flopped onto my mattress, sitting close enough for me to feel the hairs on his arm brush against my own. My parents would disapprove of a boy in my bedroom, but with them out of the picture, out of the loop, out of their minds, I invited him inside to view my artwork.

Our farmhouse sat on the outskirts of town with cornstalks on one side and trees on the remaining three. It took us a good ten minutes to walk to the road to catch the school bus back when we actually attended classes.

In our secluded stretch of land, we lacked nosy neighbors to catch Felix sneaking in through the side door. No one would gossip about us tomorrow. Inviting him inside seemed harmless. He seemed harmless.

He rubbed his fingertips across the ruffles of my skirt, the swoosh-swoosh filling the silence of my empty bedroom. I licked my lips, preparing for the kiss to come, but he challenged me to paint him instead.

"I only create landscapes," I said, eyes dropping in embarrassment. "Places I dream about visiting. I've never drawn a face before."

He browsed the row of paintings leaning up against the wall like teepees. Of Paris. Of Egypt. Of the Grand Canyon and Niagara Falls and Machu Picchu.

"You really think you'll be able to afford trips like that one day?"

"No." I shook my head, trying to get my chocolate curls to bounce like the woman in feature films, but the hair spray anchored them in place. "That would never happen."

Although I felt the heart-pull tug of a lie, I technically told the truth. I worked the farm without pay. I tended to the animals because ignoring them meant watching them die. I considered applying for a part-time job at the diner or local ice-cream shop, but my sister guilt-tripped me into changing my mind because she hated stewing in the house alone. Of course, if my parents died tomorrow, the property and everything planted in the soil went to her. I owned nothing.

"Why do you paint those places, then?" Felix asked, rising to grab a closer look.

"They're pretty," I said, hiding the truth behind a one-shoulder shrug. In earnest, the paintings started after I had sorted through a stack of books I promised myself I would never touch. My parents kept the pile inside of their bedroom but encouraged my sister and I to peruse them anytime we wanted. Rosie took them up on the offer, ferrying books into her room until her stack grew bigger than the original.

I refused to let them pass down their hobby to me, so I avoided the room at all costs. I only entered, with angry tears like bee stings in my eyes, after learning about Salem in class. A group of kids had made fun of me during the length of the lesson because my sister never stayed silent about her interest in witchcraft. They accused my family of being evil, teasing about how I would have had cinderblocks strapped to my feet one hundred years prior.

The bullying bothered me, even though I knew the difference between what the world thought magic looked like and what it really looked like in practice. "We shift luck in different directions," my mother had taught us. "We can shift luck toward our crops and they will flourish. We can shift luck away from our competition and watch them suffer a drought."

That night, I'd grabbed the first book I found and flipped through it as a research project to prove to myself we were different than the green-faced witches haunting storybooks. Amongst the spells for growing fruitful crops and earning unearned money, I found it. A transportation incantation. With the right combination of words, it would allow a person to step through a painting and into the place depicted. It would shift me away from the farmhouse and toward somewhere, anywhere, else.

Whenever my parents fought, flinging dishes and forming black eyes, I picked up a brush instead of a blade and imagined getting sucked through the image.

Even though I memorized every word on the recipe page, even though I spent most nights picturing the tastes of the outside world, I never followed the formula to completion.

If I tried to step through my favorite painting, if I used magic to solve my problems, I would be as bad as the rest of them. As much as I loved my parents, I wanted to chainsaw my branch off the family tree. I wanted to succeed without taking a shortcut. I wanted to grow old without any sins.

"If you really want me to do your portrait, I will try my best," I said to break the stretch of silence. I uncapped my paints and dipped my bristles into a milky brown, the color of Felix's skin. "As long as I get to keep it here. For my collection."

He fiddled with the collar of his checkered shirt, pretending to unbutton it. "In that case, want me to undress? Be your nude model?"

"You better sit still." I flicked my brush, scattering paint onto his sneakers. "Otherwise this isn't going to turn out well."

†

After I finished the portrait of Felix, with the nose oversized and the chin a touch too narrow, he asked me to sign my name in the corner. Like a real artist.

"Do you want to take it home?" I asked, screwing closed the lids to my paints. The rainbow set, along with the easel and palette, cost more than I could afford. It took me years to save up enough birthday money for the collection and even then I had to pawn jewelry to pay for the brushes. I suffered for my art long before my first creation.

Felix used a pinkie to test whether the canvas was dry, then kissed his painted lips with his own. "As handsome as this looks, no. You better keep it."

My heart belly-flopped. I faked a smile. Forced a nod.

"I didn't mean it as an insult. I would rather have it here." He lifted my hand. "That way, you won't forget about me. Maybe you can draw a self-portrait and I'll take that one. Then we can both see each other even when we can't see each other."

"You're cute."

"Yeah? Cute enough to be seen with in public?"

With my approval, we walked hand-in-hand to the ice-cream parlor, even though it took over an hour with the farmhouse being so detached from society. Felix ordered butterscotch with rainbow sprinkles and I stuck with vanilla, no toppings. We sword-fought with our plastic spoons and bet on which ice-cream flavor would be invented next. When a string of whipped cream dribbled onto my chin, he leaned over and wiped it off with his thumb, then stuck that thumb into his mouth.

I had met Felix in first grade, but we didn't become friends until fifth and didn't think about dating until the start of summer.

Now, it seemed like the only option. Our destined path.

We had hung out before as friends. A group of us would swap gossip in the barn or race the horses across the fields, but seeing each other one-on-one felt different. I sensed the sexual tension from the moment he arrived at my front door with his sideways smile until we said our goodbyes at the fence of the farmhouse.

With my belly filled with as much food as butterflies, the night ended with a kiss to the cheek, my lipstick an "O" against his moonlight-soaked skin.

"Next time I might let you kiss me for real," he said.

"I hope so," I said.

I crept inside three hours past curfew with his jacket hunched across my shoulders, but no figures stood at the doorway, tapping their foot in protest. No lights remained on, shining a spotlight on my irresponsibility. I pushed through the unlocked front door, tiptoed through the living room, down the extended hall, and...

I heard a thump. Coming from my room. Definitely my room.

My mind leapfrogged to the worst-case scenario. *Someone found out about the narcotics my parents created. Someone broke in to steal the supply. Someone wanted a taste for themselves.*

I shuffled back a few steps and wrestled an old picture of my sister, one from her toddler days, from off its screw. I could smash it against whoever hid inside my room and use the fallen shards as secondary weapons.

The fear took a backseat to my frustration. If my parents cared, they would have protected me. They would have heard someone tumble through the windows and silenced them with a shotgun. They would have played their role as adults instead of passing it down to their teenage children.

When I rounded the corner and stepped through my burst-open door, I lifted the picture shoulder-height, ready to swing. My eyes darted from corner to corner, searching for an intruder, but found a tornado of color instead.

From floor to ceiling, my room was splashed with red. And blue. Yellow. Green. Purple. Pink. My paints, the bottles crunched with footprints. My artwork had been shredded, pieces of Paris scattered across the floor.

My sister Rosie crouched on my bed, straddling a canvas with a knife in both hands, like she needed her full strength to swing her arm down into...

The painting of Felix. She had glued black rose petals over his eyes. Slashed him from cheek to cheek and made another slash straight down his nose like a bloodied cross.

"What are you doing? I worked hard on that," I said, letting the frame clatter to the ground and explode into sparkly chunks of glass.

"*Requiescat in pace*," she chanted over the painting. A cigarette dangled between her teeth, smudging her words. "*Omnia mors aequat.*"

"I asked you what you think you are doing."

She spit the butt onto the floor. A large wad of saliva came with it. "Never bring him here again. Never see him again."

"Never break into my room again." I tried to sound strong, but my words came out wobbly.

"I'm serious. Boys do bad things. Bad. Things. Mary."

"Get out."

"I only made him sick this time." She blinked, expressionless. "I'll kill him next time. I'll kill him to protect you."

"Get out. How many more times do you want me to say it? Three? Four?" I stepped deeper into the room, chest inflated to look defiant, hoping the darkness made the mist in my eyes invisible.

"You don't appreciate me enough," she said. "You're so ignorant sometimes."

She clacked down the halls in her slippers, leaving me to clean up glass with bare hands that bled. After dumping the shards in the trash and scrubbing paint deeper into the floors, I spent the night spilling tears over my graveyard of artwork.

Before our parents had slipped into their drug habit, back when they were the average abusive couple, Rosie and I had stuck together. We huddled in closets when they fought. We squeezed each other's hands beneath the table during uncomfortable family dinners. We acted as partners, a team.

Then, two years ago, my parents had created a concoction that nibbled at their brains, slurped at their sanity. Day after day, they dipped their needles into the mixture and pumped it into their veins, giving them an unworldly high more powerful than heroin. If they marketed it, they could have made millions.

Instead, they spent their days sleeping. Mumbling beneath their breath. Only moving to take a shit or make another dose.

Rosie took their incompetence as a sign to step into the parenting role. She became overbearing. Overprotective. She chased my friends away. She talked me out of attending school and applying for a job. She stopped holding birthday parties in the barn. She kept finding innovative ways to ruin my life. And I kept letting her.

When I cried myself into unconsciousness, I dreamt in memories. My mind replayed the whipped cream on my chin and the thumb between his lips, the ones I had come so close to kissing. Those dreams gave me five hours of peace before launching me back into reality.

I awoke to the noise of Felix's mother rattling her fist against the door. She came to tell me an ambulance had chauffeured her son to the emergency room late last night and then offered to drive me to visiting hours.

"I'm going to have to pass," I said, remembering Rosie's warning. "We're not as close as you seem to think. We're not even friends. I hope he feels better, but I'm not wasting my time going down there. You can tell him I said that."

Her jaw unhinged, disgusted that I left her son, the boy I could have loved, to rot alone.

CHAPTER III

A phone call jostles me from dreams three days after our paint class.

Before I rub the crust from my eyes to check the caller ID, before I hear the choked voice on the other side, I know my uncle has news. I know my grandmother is either wearing a hospital gown or a toe tag.

His words blend together, forming a paste that sticks in my ears like wax. *Passed peacefully. Funeral home. Could use your help.*

"I'm coming," I say with numb lips. "I'll be there."

I leave without remembering to snap on a bra or sling on my pocketbook. I drive without seeing my surroundings, my mind a blank, but somehow my muscle memory brings me to my destination.

When I climb up the broken-railed steps and push through the unlocked door, the body bag is gone. Grandma is gone. Getting her face made up one last time before her final party.

My uncle, eyelids puffed and purple, hugs the breath out of me. "She's dancing and singing in heaven with her husband right now. I'm sure the other angels are already filing noise complaints."

I hate him for joking, for shielding his emotions with humor the same way my grandmother shielded her childhood, but I follow suit. "They're probably trying to get her transferred to hell. But as long as she can have sex down there, I'm sure she's fine with it."

He burps out a laugh. "As much as it sucks, we have to figure this out sooner rather than later," he says. He arranges a deal for me to call the cousins while he calls old family friends, distant relatives, the faded names in the phonebook I don't recognize.

He also delivers the news to the nosy neighbor who walks her flabby ass over to ask about the funeral van she spotted in the driveway earlier. I listen to her clichéd sympathy through the door as she offers her *sincerest apologies* and says *if there's anything she can do…*

Grandma complained about that old hag during our drive to paint class. According to local gossip, the woman read through mail wrongly delivered to her before returning it to sender and flirted with married men at the bingo hall and couldn't even keep her own damn leaves in her yard without letting them spill over to grandma's property—but now she claims *she's in a better place.* What a bitch. What a lying little…

I launch the phone in my hand across the room and watch it smash against the wall, cracking the screen into spider webs. Chest heaving, I grab the chair back (the last chair I saw her seated on) and clutch the rail on top until the cheap wood snaps to splinters in my fist. I hurl the broken chunks against the doorway, but it collides with the painting instead. My painting. Our painting. It wobbles on its hook and then sinks to the carpet.

I crumble to the ground along with it, letting the tears roll. I hiccup from the sobs, and wet strands of hair stick in my mouth, choking me.

Did *she* choke? Did she suffocate? Did she suffer for even a second before slipping away *peacefully*? Did she have time to think about the family who would mourn her or the family she would join in the afterlife? Did she fight to hold on a little longer, or was she willing to let the Reaper curl his bone-white claws around her?

My uncle fiddles with the screen door as it closes, clattering a little too loud, warning me of his approach. Silently asking me to pull myself together so he can save the she's-in-a-better-place speech and awkward hug.

I use my wrist as a tissue, smearing the tears into my skin until they turn invisible. "It's a little early to call everyone," I say when he enters, bags hung low beneath his eyes. "I'll go through her closet until then. Find her an outfit. And pictures. We need a bunch for those bulletin boards the funeral home sets up. Then we'll have to take care of the food. People will want to stop over."

He rubs his head, his fingers tracing the curve where his hairline sat twenty years earlier. "Yeah, okay," he says as if that constitutes an answer. He sighs so deeply it turns into a cough.

I nod a silent goodbye and dip into grandma's bedroom on a search for her finest clothes. I flip through hangers of silk and lace until I find the olive-green dress, camisole, and cross she wore every birthday. I add a pair of ballet flats and sheer tights to the pile, unsure if they will bother to squeeze them onto her stiff legs when the coffin stays closed beneath the waist.

I place the outfit on the bed like an invisible body is resting there, with her necklace on the pillow and dress slung across the comforter, but the photographs prove harder to find.

Frames dangle from her walls and perch on her nightstand,

frozen moments of the cousins playing touch football on the front lawn and eating pizza with strands of cheese clinging to our chins and opening up presents beneath a white ornamented tree.

Deep in the closet, I discover yearbooks, but the sepia class pictures belong to my mother and her siblings. I find no trace of my grandmother's dimpled cheeks and blonde bangs. No snapshots of her tossing horseshoes with high-school friends or tipping back beers on the hood of her old Camaro.

I retrieve my phone from the dining room and scour social media, finding a smattering of family photographs with grandma in her later days. Bending over my baby crib. Posing with me in Halloween costumes. Hugging me during graduation day. But not one picture from her childhood or even from under the age of fifty.

I plan to check the basement for a box of albums, but I eyeball her bedroom one last time. Underneath the mattress, I find an emergency bedpan and two hard candies with fuzz stuck to the swirls. A quick check inside her dresser drawers reveals oversized underwear, limp bras with the wires poking through, and stray quarters thrown across the fabric.

A red box sits atop her dresser, flanked by her voodoo dolls wrapped in a rainbow of colors. I lift the first doll, two sticks wrapped with yellow fabric and tied with white string. When I place the doll back into position, I realize the platform it leans against holds a latch that has been painted over to disguise it.

I pry at the lock with the tips of my fingernails, chipping my black polish, but rust holds it in place. A half-peeled bee sticker stares at me from the edge, one I must have placed with grubby kid fingers a decade back.

As a toddler, my grandmother called me honey along with the rest of the grandkids. The nickname evolved in middle school, back when my dirty mind emerged. She called me *sweet as honey with a sting like a bee.* The rest of the cousins stayed grouped together with their generic pet name. No one called me out on being the favorite, but it must have run through their minds. My grandmother made her bias obvious.

At last, the latch buckles. When I reach my hands inside, I find a yellowed piece of paper smothered in dust. The looped handwriting contains a list of ingredients. The label on top reads *Transportation Incantation.*

CHAPTER IV

MARY

JULY 10, 1966

I used a piece of string snapped from the hem of a childhood dress to split the tip off my red lipstick. I placed the chunk of color inside a container I'd swiped from beneath the kitchen counters, planning to leave it in the summer sun. Melt it down to use as paint.

No matter what my sister did, no matter how many easels she splintered and rainbows she blackened, I refused to abandon my art. If I had to razorblade my skin apart and dab my brush into the wound, I would.

"You better not be naked," Rosie said from the echoing hall, causing me to sling a blanket over the hill of makeup. "I'm coming inside."

She took my silence as an invitation, barging through the threshold and dropping a handwritten list onto my lap.

"I need you to help me gather," she said with a rare smile. "I'm working on a new recipe."

I flashbacked five years, picturing the last time I helped her gather. Kids at school had found out about the marks across my back and started calling me Kitty, forming their fingers into cat claws whenever I passed. My sister had seen the scene and scribbled down a list of ingredients on the basketball court in chalk.

I'd captured three live beetles, plucked five mushrooms, and collected sap from a cluster of trees we used as home base during tag. After I'd scampered back, palms overflowing, my sister combined the ingredients with a few extras from her backpack, ground them into a dust, and blew it into one of the bullies' faces. With one whiff, he dropped onto all fours and meowed like a barn cat. The show only lasted five minutes, but it gave everyone's tiny attention spans enough time to forget about me.

"It's sort of an apology," Rosie said with words like smelling salts, bringing me back to reality. "For the other night. I can be a real bitch sometimes."

I lifted the list, skimmed it. Jasmine. Hemlock. A chicken foot. A crow feather. A lock of hair. An ounce of blood.

"What does this do?" I asked, deadpan.

"It's for mom and dad. It will help them."

"With what?"

"You want them to stop drinking, don't you? And give up the needles?"

My forehead scrunched. My eyebrows joined. "You can actually make a cure for that?"

"I never knew about it until a few days ago. I think they hid it from me on purpose. They didn't want me to know as much as them."

Unlikely. My mother loved to share her hobby. She had convinced my father to marry her by brewing a love potion and slipping it into his drink during their senior dance. They held a courthouse wedding two months later and spent every weeknight pouring through leather-bound books together. They learned cleaning spells and cooking spells. Spells to help them gain wealth and beauty, success and stronger orgasms.

When my sister had dropped from the womb, they encouraged her to study the books, quizzing her on Latin each night. They repeated the process with me, except I had resisted. Unless Rosie asked for help. I never told her *no*.

"I don't want to get the chicken foot," I said, flinching at the thought of taking an axe to a bird. "But I can get a feather. And I think most of the herbs are left in the cupboards."

She smiled. Wide. Toothy. Yellow. "I'll meet you in my room in an hour then? Ugh, it'll be so nice once mom and dad stop acting like slobs."

She padded out of the room, and after leaving my lipsticks in a puddle of sunshine on my windowsill, I went gathering. Not out of fear or familial obligation, but out of love. Love for my parents, who deserved a second chance at living above the influence. Love for myself, who spent nights fantasizing about our family reforming into something functional. Even love for my sister, who grew up alongside me, who helped raise me. She mistreated me, she isolated me, she shoved me away from my friends, but my parents made their own mistakes, and my love for them never wavered.

I dipped into the kitchen, trailing my fingers across the growth chart in the entryway. The notches carved into the wood kept track of my height until freshman year of high school. My mother had yelled at us for taking scissors to the walls back when she had enough brain cells left to notice. She had lectured us about leaving water glasses on the wooden table without a coaster, about trailing our muddy boots across the wooden floors, about digging nails into the wood-paneled walls.

Now, stray bottles littered the countertops, picture frames swung wildly from the hallways, boots dribbled water through the planks, and no one yelled. No one even noticed.

I stood on tiptoes and creaked open the cabinets above the sink. Cardboard boxes held our cluttered collection of ingredients. One for shells and one for seeds. One for twigs and one for leaves. We used to keep one for beetles and feathers and eggs but decided to find them fresh.

I stuffed the necessary herbs into the front pouch of my backpack, the same backpack where I secretly kept my transportation incantation materials, pausing by the woodblock of knives. Rosie would have nabbed one to mutilate a crow, but I planned on scouring the yard for a stray feather. I would climb trees and dig through nests for days before dismembering a living, breathing creature.

I slipped out the side door, leading from the kitchen to the horse stables, and swept my eyes across the blackened grass. Like my parents had done when they were sober, Rosie used a spell to keep the crops on the other side of the house alive but never bothered to use a similar spell on the grass. Too much trouble for a purely aesthetic purpose.

When it came to the animals, we never took shortcuts. We took turns collecting eggs and brushing horses and slopping dinner into troughs. For someone who seemed to hate all of humanity, Rosie sure loved animals. At the same time, she had no problem slaughtering them when they became a problem.

Only days earlier, I had run to her, tears misting my eyes, because a pig we fattened since childhood had fallen ill. Rosie stomped outside, ushered the pig to an empty clearing, and swung an axe through its belly. No hesitation.

I didn't even have the stomach to pull away the corpse. I left it there to rot. Like I left Felix.

Refocusing on the task at hand, it only took me fifteen minutes to find a feather swishing through the air. I caught it between pinched fingers. Considered it an offering from the gods. A sign to proceed with the spell.

I wore a light smile on my face as I returned to the house, clicking the kitchen lock in place and making my way down the hall.

"Rosie, are you back yet?" I asked, pressing my pinkie against her bedroom door to inch it open. She had asked me to meet her inside, but the last time she granted me visiting rights to her room, we were still in single digits. I never dared to step inside without her permission, so I waited for her to climb off her bed and open the door the rest of the way.

When I entered, none of the childhood drawings I remembered sat on her walls, none of the old toys ducked beneath her bed. Her windows yawned open, cigarette butts trailing down the sill like clinging vomit. A pile of burnt matches made a teepee on her rug. A matchbook stuck out from her desk drawer like a tongue. The only splash of color came from her dresser, which glittered with a knife collection.

After we pooled everything onto Rosie's floor, I watched her sprinkle and stir and speak slivers of Latin. *Nemo ante mortem beautus. Bibere venenum in auro. Extinctus amabitur idem.*

"What do those words mean?" I asked.

"It doesn't translate into English well."

A short answer. A false answer.

Like my parents, Rosie knew how to lie, manipulate, and cheat the system. She gave substitute teachers fake names and boys fake numbers with a smolder that promised they could trust her. When dad had still cared enough to discipline us, Rosie found a way to wiggle out of every single time-out. She never pinned the shattered mirrors or stolen cigarettes on me, the kid sister, the easy target. She never expected me to take the fall for her.

"Come on," she said once the mixture had thickened into a bubbling, lime-green paste. Cradling the bowl in her arms like a baby, she soft-stepped down the hall, across the kitchen, and into the living room where our parents snored.

She hovered over their unconscious bodies, dipped her finger knuckle-deep into the liquid, and painted a skinny cross on our mother's forehead. She repeated the process with our father, only pausing when their faces twitched, when they showed signs of waking.

"Can't you just tell them what you're doing?" I said. "They should be fine with it. They should want to get better. Don't you think?"

"If they did, they would have tried already. Addicts don't want to change for the better. They only get worse." A beat. "Dad's been getting worse."

Her lips hung open, weighty words on the edge of her tongue, threatening to slip off. She clamped her jaw shut before they could reach me, her teeth snapping, her pupils rising.

They followed the path of my mother, now on her feet. Her eyes rid of red. Her walk free of stumbles.

I chewed on my lip to hold back a smile. With my parents clean, I could invite friends over without worrying about them tripping across used needles. I could bring my parents to school plays and art shows without fear of being embarrassed by them. I could walk through the house on flat feet instead of tiptoes, without worrying the slightest sound might set them off like when we were kids.

"Mom," I said, trailing her into the kitchen where she walked at zombie pace. "How do you feel?"

She floated toward the island like strings pulled at her joints. No tick of the lips or twist of the head to show she had heard me.

"Mom," I repeated as her hands fumbled across the wooden countertop, fingertips flailing, like a blind woman relying on her sense of touch.

"What are you looking for?" I asked. With no response, I swiveled toward my sister. "What is she looking for? What is she doing?"

Rosie dipped her head, refusing to meet my eyes, her bangs working as a barrier to shield half her face. I hadn't heard her go quiet like that since…

I had never heard her go quiet like that.

"What is going on?" I said, returning my attention to my mother, who had finally groped something with her bone of a hand.

A handle. A knife.

She slid it from its sheath, grazed the blade with her thumb, and traded it for a larger one.

"Mom? Mom, please." I pulled at her arm, tugging it toward me, but her muscles stayed rigid, tight, taut. "Mom."

She twisted the handle until the blade aimed toward her neck, the point leaving a dimple in her flesh.

I pulled harder, harder, both hands clamping onto her forearm, but she won. She sliced through the sagging wrinkles of her throat, shredding the flesh from left to right. Warm blood spurted from the wound. The knife clattered from her limp grasp. When she collapsed onto the floor, I lost my grip on her skin. I stood silent. I stood frozen.

My father must have lifted from his chair through the chaos, because now he shuffled toward his bride, bent to search for the knife she had dropped with a blind man's grope, and wrenched the blade into his chest. It stayed there, poking out from his severed heart, as he thumped onto the floor, side-by-side with my mother, in the same way they would be positioned in their coffins.

I sunk onto the floor with them, too confused for the tears to come. Confused about the spell. Confused about the suicide.

Confused about why Rosie had avoided glancing at mom when she had plunged the blade into her body but looked straight at dad when he had done the same.

CHAPTER V

I twist the key to my apartment door and step into the clutter. Unmatched shoes stack against the wall. Boxed wine sits on the countertop. My undergraduate schedule sticks to the fridge with a mustache-shaped magnet, reminding me how soon until winter break ends.

I excavate my laptop from a mountain of paperwork, sit cross-legged on my unmade bed, and Google the words atop the sheet I'd found in my grandmother's bedroom: Transportation Incantation.

The page explains the steps to traveling through a painting and into the place depicted.

According to the faded loops of script, five ingredients are required before I can use the spell. One squeeze of lemon. One splash of jasmine. One clove of hemlock. Grocery-store items.

The next ingredient leans more toward *complicated*. "An item from the physical location portrayed inside of the painting."

Unable to think about the impending funeral without bursting back into my ugly cry, I kept my focus on the list of ingredients while I dialed my cousins to deliver the news and ordered coleslaw for the reception. I moved out of muscle memory but was only half-there. While I spoke, I went through ingredient options in my mind, debating what best represented the farm-house, and settled on the horseshoe my grandmother kept above her entryway, the one facing toward the heavens for good luck. I remembered her saying it belonged to a horse from her stables. Pieces of earth, molecules of life, could still be stuck in the crevices from the time it spent galloping across the property.

If I ended up tipsy enough test out the spell, the horseshoe would help. Not that the rational part of my brain believed the incantation would work as advertised. Not even my grief could make me that gullible.

I swiped it anyway. Stuffed it into the waist of my jeans and drove back to my apartment with it just in case.

Now, in the safety of my bedroom, I toss the horseshoe across my blankets like a Frisbee and flick my eyes over the paper one more time. The final step involves splitting my flesh into a thin line and letting a few drops of blood spill out. The rest of the ingredients would be blended together, mixed with the horse-shoe working as a whisk. After that, I would smear the concoction over the painting in the form of a triquetra (Google defined it as a symmetrical triangular ornament of three interlaced arcs, meant to represent the Holy Trinity) and speak the incantation.

When I slip a jacket over my shoulders and punch the nearest grocery store into my GPS, I ask myself why. My grandmother collected totems, she believed in superstitions, but she discouraged witchcraft. She scrounged together enough money to buy me a designer bag for my sixteenth birthday, a pocketbook that cost more than that month's mortgage, but she refused to give me twenty bucks for the magic kit I kept seeing on commercials as a kid, and when a friend bought me a Ouija board, she dug through my bag for the receipt to return it. "Dark magic is for dark souls," she said, and I argued with her about her voodoo doll family. She said not to talk about them, that adults are complicated, that they are allowed to act hypocritical.

She would disapprove of me completing the recipe, even as a way to distract myself, even as a way to keep me from getting blackout drunk to cope with my loss.

The devil inside me disagreed. It convinced me she kept the page for a reason. Maybe she saved it as a way for me to find the answers to questions I spent my life asking. Or a way for me to give a proper goodbye.

†

I place a butter knife on my bed, along with a razorblade, pocket-knife, and steak knife, unsure of which one will get the job done without causing an infection or cutting too deep or not scraping deep enough.

Back in our teen years, one of my cousins burnt herself with her hair curler and left slices across her forearms but blamed the marks on random incidents. Cat scratches. Scrapes from the thorn bush lining her porch steps. Nicks from the disposable razor balanced on her bathtub.

When she told the rest of the cousins the truth one tipsy Thanksgiving, about how she felt numb and the pain electrocuted her back to life, everyone nodded along except me. Everyone understood except me.

"Eeny, meeny, miny, moe…" I bounce my finger from one item to the next, settling on a plastic pink razor. I pop the blade from its stem, rest the edge against my upper arm, and apply pressure. A little deeper. A little harder. Not enough to send me to the ER, but enough to break the flesh.

When I ease the blade off to examine the mark, my freckled skin looks baby-smooth. No blood. Not even a white scrape line.

"Damn it." I sigh, pounding a fist against my sheets to cause a ripple. "I can't…damn it."

I cast my mind back to my cousin, my model-beauty cousin who secretly felt numb, who left slashes across her skin to feel a sliver of pain, a stab of normalcy.

My pain elicits the opposite reaction. Numbness sounds like more of a relief than a curse. I already feel too much. Too human. Too broken. Too bashed. *Too much too much too much.*

In one swoop, I press the razor into my flesh until the fat spills over the metal. I flick my wrist to the right, retaining the pressure, as it skids off my arm and into the damp air.

"G'ahhh."

A pause, a brief flutter in time, and the blood emerges. It bubbles from my flesh for a few seconds and then leaks in faucet-like waves, leaving watery streaks down to my elbow.

I hover my arm over the container, letting it drip drip drip into the mixture. When it turns a light pink, I swirl the horseshoe through the ingredients once, twice, three times, and then tilt myself toward the painting propped against my headboard. Using my thumb, I make the first part of the triquetra, the top section, and dip my finger back into the warmth of the bowl. I create more lines, rounded lines, connected lines, and wonder whether my work is worthy of sacrilege.

My body urges me to reach for a towel, a bed sheet, a sock, anything to plug the wound. But the final part of the recipe remains. A Latin phrase, translated to mean *here we will stay, most excellently.*

With a glance at my grandmother's diary, I say, "*Hic manebimus optime.*"

Seconds tick. My mouth twists to the side. I wonder if I pronounced every word properly, if I put the emphasis in the correct places. "*Hic manebimus optime,*" I say again, altering my accents.

When nothing changes, I part my lips to speak one last time— until I notice the blood on my thighs rising into the air and hovering, like a solid piece of string being lifted by an invisible hand. The hair around my shoulders lifts as well, up and up and up into the air like I jammed my finger into a socket.

My arms extend next. They both float into a Frankenstein pose, level with my chest. No amount of force convinces them to lower. My muscles no longer belong to me.

By the time my feet and legs and torso lift, a group effort, I realize I am floating toward the painting. The *growing* painting, its reach expanding by the second. Or am I shrinking? The baby-blue farmhouse, which used to be the size of a light bulb, sprouts to the size of my window. My wall. My entire apartment.

I drift closer and closer to the life-size painting until we are about to collide. When we do, I feel a splat to indicate the separation between present and painting, the gap between this reality and that one.

My nose scrunches, level with my cheeks. My chest flattens. My bones crunch. My skull collapses in on itself.

A tingle swarms through me, evacuating my mind, excavating my thoughts. My vision explodes with whiteness. My mouth goes numb. My hearing melts away. All five senses, gone in a heartbeat.

Then there is a *pop*. My skull inflates. My bones rejoin. My chest puffs out. My nose pops back.

When my eyelids unfold, white swirls dangle from a purple sky. My back presses against overgrown grass.

I hear whinnies and chirps, oinks and caws, the noises of the farmhouse.

CHAPTER VI

MARY

JULY 10, 1966

I sat on folded knees, my denim tie-dyed red, my sleeves sopping with blood. I had tried beating my fists against my mother's ribcage, spitting air into her mouth, and clamping the cut with my hands to slow the gushing. Anything to zap energy back into her pulse.

Nothing worked. Her lungs emptied. Her eyes tightened. Her heart went silent inside her.

When I found the strength to stand, Rosie thrust a shovel into my hands. "Come on. We have to bury them before their bodies start to stink up the place." She blanketed our mother with a tarp found beneath the sink but left our father stripped, bare, vulnerable. "I considered chopping them up and feeding them to the pigs, but that seemed like too much work."

"How can…I'm not going to…." My mouth snapped open and closed, a fish gasping for a breath. "I'm calling the police."

"We're not involving any cops." She took a protective step toward the corded phone on the counter, legs braced. "They'll throw you in foster care if you rat. You have to keep quiet. No one will notice they're gone. They don't work. They don't shop. They don't leave the house."

"That doesn't mean they deserve to die."

"It means no one will miss them."

"Except for me."

She rolled her eyes to the ceiling.

"Rosie. You know this is wrong. You know because you would have told me the truth otherwise. You made me think we were fixing them. You didn't mention anything about a suicide spell because you can hear it. You can hear how screwed-up those words sound together." A pause to lick my cracked lips, to catch my lost breath. "What was the point? Of any of it?"

"I told you I would fix them. And I did. I fixed everything for you."

"Why, though? You're almost eighteen. You can leave soon. You can leave right now. You don't have to see them ever again. Why would you risk—"

"Because you turn sixteen this week," she said shrill, shaky, scared. Like my birthday meant something. Like my age mattered somehow.

"Our parents are dead. You are a murderer. If you want to keep me from calling the cops and getting your butt locked up in prison, I think I deserve a little more of an explanation than that."

"I hurt them before they could hurt us. What else do you need to know?"

"They barely moved. They never even argued with each other anymore. Our birthdays are the only time when they even bother to…"

"Mary." She paused for long enough to close her eyes and sip in a few shallow breaths. "You are either going to help me dig these two graves or I will dig three on my own."

With that, she disappeared out the door, shovel scraping

against the wooden planks. I flung my own shovel against the wall and watched it bounce before disappearing into my bedroom, locking the door, and jamming a chair under the handle as an extra precaution. Not strong enough to stop magic but sturdy enough to buy time if Rosie rammed inside.

After swiping stray tears with my knuckles, I grabbed my containers of melted lipstick and placed them within an arm's length of my easel. I drowned my brush in the red liquid, attempting to paint a pile of leaves, but the consistency made my lines clotted and clumpy. Unusable.

For my next attempt, I used the remainder of my lipstick tube like a pencil to paint something basic, a sun, but the lines came out too thick, like a marker with a fat tip.

I considered tunneling through junk drawers for a pen my parents hadn't converted into narcotic tubes, but my sketches never came out the same as my paintings. Lead felt different in my hands than a paintbrush.

Like Goldilocks, I refused to settle for too big or too small, too thin or too plump. Nothing felt *just right* except for my brush.

Frustrated, I hurled my makeup out the window, one piece after another. Without Felix, painting my face felt meaningless anyway.

The thoughts of him stewing in a hospital bed worsened my anxiety, causing me to collapse onto my bedroom floor. If I snuck into town to buy more paints, Rosie would assume the trip concerned the police and would conjure up a new spell to ship me off with our parents. But without those paints, creating an accurate enough portrait for a transportation incantation would prove impossible. I would never escape. I would never outrun my sister. I would never find out if the damn spell even worked.

CHAPTER VII

When I crunch myself into a sitting position, the first thing I see are four stubby feet sticking in the air. A pig flopped on its back with flies swarming around its open belly. I swallow the bullet of vomit shooting up my throat and remind myself where I am—away from the heart of Long Island and in a tight corner of Tennessee. On farms, animals get slaughtered for Thanksgiving dinners, for summer barbeques, for breakfast sandwiches. Death is welcomed here.

"Hey! What the hell?"

My hand springs against my heart to keep it jammed in place. My fingers brush against the cellphone in my breast pocket and I make a mental note to avoid drawing attention to the bulge.

"Who are you?" a teenage voice says, piercing through the quiet. She holds a shovel with the spade facing toward me like a spear. "What are you doing on our property?"

At sloth speed, I rise to my feet, keeping my arms extended and fingers splayed. "I'm sorry. I didn't mean to trespass."

"Did you mean to avoid answering my question?"

"Sorry," I say again, stumbling for an answer. Back in my bedroom, I never dreamt of the incantation working. I expected to fail, hate myself for graffitiing my grandmother's final creation, and punish myself by drowning in whatever whiskey remained beneath my sink.

"I don't need an apology." She heaves the shovel higher, preparing to swing. "I need an explanation."

If my grandmother—is this girl my grandmother? or her friend? or a relative?—hears the truth and dubs me crazy, the trip becomes pointless. It robs me of the chance to learn the truth of her childhood.

Aiming for her sentimental side, I rub at the blood on my arm, drawing attention toward it. "I've been running from my family. I need a place to stay. Thought a farm would be nice and big. Room for a stranger. I could sleep with the horses. Just can't go back home. Not yet. Not ever maybe."

She eyes me, from my scoop-neck shirt to my torn jeans and fur-lined boots. Dressed for warmer weather, she wears a thin orange shirt with denim capris and sneakers.

"Are you running because you did something or they did?" she asks.

"I didn't do anything illegal if that's what you mean. I've never even been grounded before. Or gotten detention. I'm a good kid. Too good. Other kids hated me."

"Good kids usually have friends they can stay with."

I force my shoulders into a shrug. "Their family would call mine. They would say where I was hiding. I didn't want to risk it."

"You only want to stay here for a night? Then you'll get going?"

"Yes."

"I don't know if I believe you," she says, lowering the shovel to the ground. "But you look like you're in trouble. So as long as you're not any trouble for me, I'll let you stay in my room for a night. Just one. My sister can't find out or it'll be bad. Okay?"

She leads me through acres of overgrown grass, past a barn with whinnies squeezing through the wooden panels, and toward a two-story house with pale blue shutters. The long walk gives me a chance to look at her, at least from behind. Her hair seems darker than my grandmother wore it in old age, but it holds the same thick curls. She walks with a teenager's caution, a bowed head that swivels back and forth, looking for signs of trouble. She makes me duck past a row of windows and when I crouch, I notice the dirt staining her pants, along with something red.

"Is that blood?"

"Paint," she says a little too quickly.

"Oh, really? Are you repainting walls? Decorating?"

"Not that kind of painting. I use an easel."

Before old age snatched my grandmother's mind, she painted watercolors and acrylics, sewed scarves, crocheted blankets, folded origami. On birthdays, she set up sand art or perler beads for everyone at my parties to work on. She encouraged arts and crafts. She told me she liked the idea of making something out of nothing. *Maybe that's why I had so many kids,* she joked.

"So you're an artist?" I ask. "You're creative?"

I keep my voice casual, but the question underneath is: *Am I right? Are you her? Am I with you again?*

She nods, dimples outlining the edges of her lips. I imagine her sixty years older, smiling a copycat smile with fewer teeth and more gum. Two conflicting feelings collide inside my mind. *I miss my grandmother* and *I am with my grandmother.*

We maneuver through the front door, into a living room with

dark dots staining the carpet, down an extended hallway filled with dusty family photographs, and swerve a right into her bedroom. A rainbow of scribbles decorates the wall. An empty easel sits abandoned in the corner, adjacent to a window that overlooks another section of the farm.

Staring through the frosted glass, I see cornstalks swaying in the wind. Chickens pecking past. The sun cresting over the horizon. No wonder my grandmother learned to paint with so much to see from her own window. Whenever I peer out the small slits in my apartment, my options are admiring the paint-tagged alleyway or the steaming row of dumpsters.

"You have a lot of land," I say. "You must have to drive for miles to reach the schoolyard."

She bolts the lock on her door and shuts the blinds on the window. "Not anymore. We used to go, but now we have lessons at home. At least, in theory. I can't remember the last time I learned something unless I picked up a book myself."

"That sounds pretty boring. Do you at least have friends that come over?"

"I used to have people visit every weekend. And we had these big parties for our birthdays each year in the barn, but this past year our parents kind of....They got really sick. And my sister became super-protective. She started scaring away my friends. So I can't really invite anyone over anymore."

My grandmother never mentioned a sister before. Our family assumed she grew up with brothers. Muscle for the farm. Of course, we also assumed the foster system separated her from her siblings before she hit double digits, another miscalculation. After fewer than five minutes on the farmland, I realized we knew less than we thought about her. We knew nothing at all.

"Is your birthday soon?" I ask when I realize I have been silent too long, staring at her features and imagining age molding her into the grandmother I recognize.

"Tomorrow. I'm turning sixteen."

I do the math in my head. That makes it late in the 1960s. "Are you upset you aren't going to celebrate?"

"Not really. I always felt like they were apology parties."

"Apologies for what?"

"My parents are into…it sounds crazy to say out loud, but they're into blood magic. Every birthday, they take some from us. My sister loves spells, too, and even she hates the ritual."

My skin prickles with goose bumps. "They would use needles, like a nurse?"

"A knife. They would turn us over and slit our backs with it."

My eyes saucer, but I don't want to come across as repulsed and scare her into keeping the story to herself. "Why, though? What's the point?"

"They saved the blood in jars. For certain incantations. When they wanted us to sleep for days so they could take a vacation alone, they'd use our blood as an ingredient, because it helped the spell last longer. When we got older, they stopped using magic on us, but they kept the jar ritual. Like some people trim their trees on Christmas, I guess."

"You couldn't ask them to stop? Or have your sister talk to them?"

"My sister is worse than they are. She made my boyfriend sick, but I thought it was because she was jealous. She's never brought a boy back home before. But then she…our parents are dead because of her."

My mind skips back to every time I questioned my grandmother about her childhood. Every time I grew frustrated with her dodging the topic, begging to learn more about my family tree. I never should have pried. I should have respected her privacy.

"That's actually why I'm letting you stay here," she says. "I was thinking you could do me a favor. You owe it to me."

"What do you need?"

"When you leave here, go to the police. Tell them there are two dead bodies at the blue farmhouse. They'll know where you mean. If you're worried they'll bring you back to your parents or something, then you can call them anonymously instead. I have payphone money."

My heart twists in its ribcage, hating myself for lying to her. I am tempted to blanket her in a bear hug, to remind her she is loved, to assure her everything is going to work out okay because her family in the future will make up for her family of the past.

I chew on a flaking piece of my lower lip, wondering whether giving her such significant information would disrupt the timeline, whether the future would change based on my presence alone or whether the story was always written this way.

Part of me expects everything to snap back into place once I leave. I think of my invasion as a peek into the past, one where I am incapable of committing lasting damage. I see myself as a spectator. A woman watching a film, able to yell directions at the characters but aware my advice won't change their actions.

Another part of me thinks that I have more influence than I should. That I am a catalyst.

I thrust the competing thoughts from my mind, accept my ignorance, and choose the easiest solution. To lie.

"Yeah. I can do that for you," I say. "Of course I will."

She nods, a silent thank you, but immediately changes the conversation. "Where did you say you're from again?"

I give her a fake last name and complain about my barbarous, nonexistent brothers. I sprinkle in half-truths about my absentee father deserting me as a fetus and my mother dying from cancer in my teens and my grandmother taking over as my mother figure, raising me as her own.

When I finish patching my story together, I say, "I'm Gillian, by the way. I think we know everything about each other except for names."

"That's true. I guess we worked backwards." I earn a tinkling laugh from her. It holds more helium than in her old age. "I'm Mary."

My grandmother never uttered her birth name. She introduced herself as Catherine to the ladies at her church, Cathy to neighbors, and Kate to cute mailmen and cashiers. One Easter, after too many Schaefer's, she pulled me to the side and admitted she changed her name as a teenager. I jumped to cinema-level conclusions, assuming the witness protection program transferred her from her home after getting too close to a crime or serving on a jury.

I never imagined she came from a family she dreamt of escaping from forever. I never pictured her with a pack slung over her back, sneaking away from the people who raised her, but now I do.

It makes me miss her even more, even though a version of her stands in front of me, stealing glances at the closed door, flinching at every unfamiliar sound. A stab of longing pierces my chest because she is protecting me now the same way she protected me throughout childhood before our roles swapped. Before she became a countdown to a corpse.

"What's wrong?" she asks, bending her fingers around my shoulder. The concern etched into her cheeks brings me to the realization that tears are sloshing across my own. I touch my fingertips against the wetness and look down at them like I'm checking for blood.

"Sorry." I blink the tears dry. "Leaving home hasn't been the easiest. I just miss my family, I guess."

"Missing them doesn't mean you're meant to be with them, though," she says, squeezing twice, comforting me about her own death.

CHAPTER VIII

MARY
JULY 11, 1966

It took until sunrise to finish carving a hole into the ground and rolling our parents inside like fat sacks of manure. During the process, I had played nice with Rosie. I wore a plastic smile, pretended to agree with her psychopathic plan, and swore not to visit the cops. She trusted me enough to loosen her tether. By the time we finished our excavation, she let me wander off on my own while she disappeared into the shower.

With no hope of sleeping, I had planned on collecting eggs, throwing slop in the pig trough, and brushing the horses at record speed to give me time to sneak onto my bike. If I sped down to the police station without Rosie noticing me missing, officers would handcuff her before she had time to punish me for breaking my word. She had already disconnected the phone lines, severing them with a pair of scissors at the risk of being electrocuted, so flagging someone down face-to-face seemed like my only hope.

Unfortunately, I never had the chance to attempt my escape, because a young woman with blood running down her arm stumbled across the lawn before I could store my shovel in the shed. When she explained her situation, her pupils darted here to there, signaling a lie, but I agreed to share my room in exchange for a favor. Inviting a stranger into our home felt like less of a risk than spending the night alone with Rosie.

Soon after we reached the cavity of my room, I had spilled everything to her. About my sister. About my parents. About their corpses. It felt like therapy. A long-needed release.

Revealing lifelong secrets to a complete stranger should have felt like a betrayal to the people who raised me, but I had been loyal to them for long enough. Besides, the more the girl knew, the more she would tell the police and the quicker they would come down here.

I planned on sending her away after the sun dropped while Rosie practiced spells inside her bedroom, situated away from the windows closest to the road. Until then, I ordered Gillian to remain trapped inside my own room.

"I'll be gone for a little bit. Don't say a single word. Don't even talk to yourself," I told her as I tugged on my sneakers and slung on my backpack, preparing for my morning of chores. Still half-asleep, she mumbled about how she never woke up before noon unless it was for a *walk of shame.*

Used to the early hours, I heaved hay into a wheelbarrow and scattered chunks across the ground so the horses would chew on it instead of the dead grass. After that, I cleaned out the water troughs and refilled them with fresh water from the well. I shoveled up the manure, spent a little time brushing manes, and moved onto the pigs.

We kept them in a separate pen, a large one, so they had room to splash in their baby pool and roll their bellies in the sand. I fed them food smelling of vomit, cleaned their dirtied beds, and circled around to the other side of the house to collect eggs.

I saved the chickens for last because we both hated the coop. We needed to bend to fit inside. Rosie even resorted to crawling after her incident. One time she tripped over a runaway chicken, smashed her head against a nesting box, and came away with a bloody slash through her eyebrow. I had asked her whether she could use magic to fix it, but she said without pain she would become weak, so she let it scab.

I finished with the chickens as quickly as I could, and when it came time to cook, I cracked an extra egg into a pan for breakfast, snuck a plate under the door for Gillian, and joined Rosie at the table like every Monday.

"I feel more comfortable here already," she said between bites of bacon. "I should have used that incantation months ago."

I clamped down my frustration, stuffed it deep into my stomach. I needed to play the part of the reliable, nonthreatening sister to avoid rousing her suspicions. If she sniffed out the truth, she would never give me the freedom to leave the farmhouse. I would never have the chance to contact the police.

"Nothing really feels different for me," I said. "Before this, we cooked. We cleaned. We fed the animals. We were always the adults in this house, even when they were here."

She nodded, pleased to have me on her side, and went into a spiel about the new incantations she planned to test soon.

When she finished her meal, she slid her leftovers into the garbage but paused with her foot on the pedal. She stared into the hole with a tilted head, scrunching her lips to one side, then the other. Finally, she lifted a shell with the tip of her pinkie finger.

"Why are there three eggshells in the trash?"

I sipped my orange juice, ransacking my brain for a believable lie. "I dropped one on the floor before."

"I don't see a stain."

"I wiped it up."

"You wiped it up?"

"If you're mad at me for wasting them, I collected six more from the coops just this morning. We should be good for the week."

She blinked at me long and slow. I heard the change in her chest from across the room, her relaxed breathing shifting into something hard, deep, wheezy. "Is Felix back?"

"What?"

"Answer the question."

"I couldn't even invite him over if I wanted him here." I failed to keep the spice out of my voice. "He's still in the hospital because of you."

Rosie kicked at the trashcan. It wobbled, then toppled. "There are three eggshells in the trash. Three plates missing from the drying rack. Why did you make three portions, Mary Elizabeth?"

Her fingers rolled into balls. Her lips puckered into circles. I considered hitting her with more lies, but she would see through them. I needed to deliver the truth. I needed to rat out Gillian.

My thumb rubbed at a notch in the coffee cup, flicking off flakes. "It's not Felix."

"Liar."

"It's a girl."

"You wouldn't be hiding a girl. It's a boy. You brought a boy into your bedroom. What the hell is wrong with you?"

I kept my voice feather-light, my features soft as clay. I hoped holding my composure would rub off on her, prevent her from doing anything impulsive. "I found her on our property yesterday. She ran away from home. She needed a place to stay. I'll kick her out tonight if you want me to. I'll kick her out right now. Do you want me to go get her?"

Her eyes shrunk to slits. I saw the saliva slide down her throat in a hard ball. "If it's really just a girl, what's the point? You always want more people around. Felix. Mom. Dad. And now, some stranger."

"She needed a place to stay," I repeated.

"I don't want to hear about it anymore." She rustled through the cupboards, plucking out a dozen different herbs and knocking a dozen others onto the countertops. She carried the chosen ones in the scoop of her shirt like a basket. "Have fun with your friend. Let her be your new sister since I'm not enough family for you."

"Rosie. Come on."

She abandoned the kitchen and disappeared down the hallway, stomping dirty footprints into the floor along the way. I pictured her exploding into her room, flipping through her spell books until she found something new, something apocalyptic, something to make me suffer for my mistakes.

Hitching my backpack high onto my shoulders, I fled back to my bedroom to warn Gillian. She needed to leave. She needed to live.

CHAPTER IX

Even from my hiding spot, I can hear a young girl saying, "Have fun with your friend." It sounds like my grandmother without the rasp of old age.

Against Mary's wishes, I nudge her bedroom door open and peek through the slit to see the sister she warned me about. Blonde hair. Curls. A cut through the center of her right eyebrow.

It takes a second to register the sight and the knowledge that comes with it. My grandmother is not the soft-hearted painter who took me into her room, who kept me safe amongst the chaos of the farmhouse.

My grandmother is the girl who destroyed a roomful of paintings. The girl who sent an innocent boy to the emergency room. The girl who murdered her own parents. The girl who might murder me.

"I need you to leave right now," Mary says when she storms inside, the door ramming into my side from standing too close. She crosses the room, unlatches the window, and shoves her easel aside to make room for my legs to dangle through. "My sister is going to kill you. She killed my mom and dad. She's going to kill you, too. She will."

I wobble my head back and forth. "No. You can't kick me out. I'm not from here."

"You can take the bus. There's a station a few miles south. I have money. And quarters. As soon as you find a payphone, call the police. Tell them to come here."

"You don't understand. I'm from…I came here with a transportation incantation."

She falls silent. Her face freezes in a mannequin stare, like concrete has cascaded over her skull. No words escape from her opened lips. No movement occurs inside her darkened pupils.

I wonder if the truth has shattered all her trust in me, if she is counting all the lies I've told since arriving here. Will she deliver me to her sister? Insist on saving me? Throw up her hands and let me fend for myself?

"I'm related to you. I'm not born…for a while," I continue, the words soft and slow so they have time to seep into her. "I came here to visit. To see the farmhouse for myself."

She rubs circles into her forehead. "Are you my daughter? My granddaughter?" Her voice comes out as stiff as her body.

"I'm not sure if I should tell you this stuff." She waits for more while I rub my lips together like cricket legs, my mind jackhammering. If I tell her the truth, she might refuse to help me to spite her sister. She might let me die as retribution. So I make a choice.

"Granddaughter," I say. "You created a portrait of this farmhouse—it was beautiful, really—and when I found your old diary with the transportation incantation inside, I wanted to see if it worked."

"Why would you want to visit me if you could…?" She trails toward the answer. "I must have died. You must have missed me."

"The funeral is tomorrow. In my time." I scratch at my forearm, uncomfortable, but her round face rises into a smile.

"That means I live for decades. Long enough to have grandkids. I don't die here. I don't die in this goddamn farmhouse." She claps her hands together. Laughs. "Do I ever see the world? Do I get out of this state? See the places I painted in person?"

Guilt quickens my heartbeat. The stories patched together from my family were littered with plot holes. Everyone believed my grandmother came from a group of brothers torn apart from the foster system. We assumed abusive parents raised her, when in reality she was the abusive one. I knew nothing about a sister. Nothing about Mary or her future—if she even had one.

Locked into survival mode, I push the reality from my mind. In the most believable way I can muster, I say, "You live on the East Coast. In your dream house. Filled with art. You live a long life. A happy one."

She looks so relieved, so at peace, that I pray I'm telling the truth.

CHAPTER X

MARY

JULY 11, 1966

From two rooms over, we heard Rosie's temper tantrum from the kitchen. She must have returned for more materials. Metal clanged against wood. Wood thumped against marble. I could picture her flinging silverware over her shoulder and swiping appliances off the countertops. Searching for the right ingredients to punish us and making a hurricane in the process.

"Let me stall her," I said to Gillian, stumped about how in the world we would get her back to her own time and place. "Let me try to talk to her."

"What if she uses magic on you?"

"She's not a wizard. She can't wave a wand and hurt me. She would have to gather materials, brew something together, and get it into my system somehow."

"Can you do that to her? Use an incantation to, I don't know, calm her down?"

"The spell books are in her bedroom. The only one I memorized was the transportation incantation. I never wanted to use any others. I didn't want to end up like my parents."

Gillian, my granddaughter, my flesh and blood, nodded. I wondered if her deep brown eyes belonged to Felix. If we passed our genes down to a son or a daughter who went on to birth the woman in front of me. I wanted to ask her more, about my marriage and my mothering and my artwork, but I swallowed my questions. I would rather find out over time.

Fiddling with the straps on each side of my backpack, I shambled down the hall like walking the corridors in a haunted house, expecting my worst nightmare to lunge at any moment. Every few steps, I paused to listen for the shifts in sound. The clanging and clashing had stopped, allowing a new noise to emerge.

"Hmm hm-hmm hmm hm-hm."

The further I advanced, the louder the humming grew. A familiar tune. *Happy birthday.*

"Rosie, are you okay in there?" I said, crossing into our hellhole of a kitchen. Maneuvering around the whirlwind Rosie had made took work. I had to aim my steps between the sprawled pots, toppled cans, and splattered glass. Three times I tripped and caught my fall.

When I reached my sister at the table, she kept her hands on her lap, out of view, but I noticed the muscles in her arms twitching, twirling something beneath the wood. Two jars of blood were perched in front of her. Yellowed labels slapped onto the sides held our names in bubble letters.

"I never used your blood in a spell before," Rosie said, still twirling. "I figured it was about time I tried it. I could make you kill your friend. I could make you draw it out so that it's long and painful."

"That's why you ransacked this whole place? The jars? I never even knew where mom and dad kept them."

"I had to find them. It's your birthday."

She lifted her hands, revealing a curved knife speckled with dark flecks. Not the one our parents had plunged into their own bodies. The one they had used to drain our blood for over a decade.

I cast my mind back to past birthdays. Number seven when they had duct-taped my mouth to keep me from nipping. Number ten when they had ordered Rosie to hold me down because of all the kicking, but she refused and received another wound herself. Number thirteen when my willpower had faded completely and they complimented me for being so cooperative, such a *good daughter*.

"We can't break tradition." Rosie stood, kicking back her chair. It made a whining sound. "Since you miss mom and dad so bad, I'll make you feel like they're back at home. It will be like their ghosts are right in front of us." A sniffle, the sound of snot sliding up her nose. "Happy birthday, Mary."

She barreled in my direction. I flew into a protective stance, guarding my head with clenched fists, but she went for my stomach, knocking me to the ground, sucking the air from my lungs.

My backpack cushioned the fall. Without it, my back would have landed directly against a fallen vase. The tinted green glass would have forked into my skin, making a home there.

I flopped my arm out, groping for anything I could reach to defend myself. A pot. A pan. A spoon. Anything. I wrapped my fingers around the only item within reach. A damn dish towel. When she straddled me, I whipped the fabric at her face, stinging her eyes until they blinked back tears, but she recovered quickly.

She dug her knees into my thighs and clamped onto my throat

with her free hand. I wiggled my waist to escape, but she pinned me in place, panting out of anger, not strain. Twenty pounds heavier and ten times more intelligent, she held more power in every sense of the word. Any second, she could use the knife. She could kill me.

She eased up instead, only to say, "Roll over" with breath like cigarettes.

I considered listening to her, letting her flip me over, roll my shirt to my collar, and dig the knife inside to see if she called a truce after. To see if she would even go through with the blood-letting. She had never hurt me before. Never punched me on the arm or pulled my hair. Never even tickled me after I told her to stop the first time.

I decided to take the risk. To trust her.

Pieces of pottery littered the floor to my right, too far to reach as a weapon but too close to risk rolling onto and injuring myself further. The left seemed safer, so I rolled toward the table, bang-ing into one of the legs. It wobbled.

Silence. Then a crash. One of our jars had rolled off the ta-bletop. It smashed against the floor, centimeters away from us, splashing us both with cold blood.

"I can't believe you'd do that to me," she said, her voice velvet. Delicate. Hurt.

I assumed she blamed me for the bloodshed until I followed her eyes. The glass on the floor had ripped my backpack, shred-ded it down the center. She could see the items sloshing out from the pockets. The ingredients for the transportation incantation.

"You don't even like spells and you were going to use one to get away from me?" Her eyes foamed. "You were going to leave me here?"

I parted my lips to speak, but the walls of my throat were still clenched together from her chokehold. I spit out air, not words.

"You want to leave so badly? You hate this house so badly?" She rose to her feet. Rushed for the side door, stopping at a box of dried twigs that had fallen from the cabinet of ingredients.

I waited for her to toss them into a bowl. To mix them with more ingredients. To create a revenge spell.

"You're finally getting what you wanted," she said. She submerged her hand into her pocket and withdrew a single match. A cigarette followed.

After lighting the end and blasting a cyclone of smoke in my direction, she relaxed her grip, letting the fire fall from her fingertips.

I expected the flames to swallow the twigs in a single gulp, but it slurped them one at a time. A slow build. With the cigarette still clenched between her teeth, Rosie grabbed another box of ingredients and overturned it, more kindling for the pile. She smirked when the flames pulsed.

"You love this house." I stuttered through my words. "You want to lose everything you care about all at once?"

"I'd rather have a fresh start." More twigs. Some leaves this time.

"Where? Where would you even go if you didn't have this place?"

"Maybe Machu Picchu. Paris. One of those crappy places you like to draw."

My cheek twitched. "There are less dramatic ways to piss off your sister."

"I would do it to *honor* you."

"Honor my death, you mean."

"Fire purifies," she said and ducked out the side door. Disappeared from the farmhouse. From my world. In a flash like a lighter.

With her gone, unable to wrestle me to the ground if I moved toward the flames, I debated my next move. I could grab the dish towel I'd used earlier and smother the flames with it, but they had grown uncontrollable. Soon they would connect with the wooden panels on the kitchen walls. The boards would curl beneath the heat.

Refusing to watch the fallout, I scooped the loose ingredients from my backpack, grabbed the remaining jar of blood, and bolted back into my bedroom at the opposite end of the house in a race against the Reaper.

CHAPTER XI

"Are you okay? I heard a lot of crashing, I almost came to get you," I say when Mary returns, half-outside the door she ordered me to hide behind. "Did she use an incantation? It smells like burning. Does she have a cauldron?"

"The kitchen is on fire."

"Holy shit." I fish for the phone in my pocket and jab 911 into the cracked keypad. No dial tone. No bars. No service. "Fuck. Ugh. What…which door do we use?"

She ignores the phone in my hand, her focus elsewhere. "We're not leaving. Rosie's too protective of me. If we go outside, she'll see you. If she sees you, she'll kill you. We're staying here until we get you out of here. Then I'll just jump out the window or something. I'll have time."

She unfolds her crumpled easel. Props a piece of canvas against the wood.

"What is that for?" I ask. "Kindling?"

"You came here with a transportation incantation. We're going to get you out with one."

I eye the jar in her hand, swishing with crimson. Her name adorns the label in black capitalized letters. "Using blood?"

"Paints." She uncaps the jar. "I have all the ingredients ready. I was thinking of using the incantation myself. To escape. It used to be something I would think about from time to time, a day-dream I never planned on actually going through with, but after she killed our parents…I started taking the idea more serious."

"Why didn't you try it then?"

"I told you Rosie ruined my paints. I was going to use makeup as a substitute, but I was worried it wouldn't work. That the picture wouldn't come out accurately enough."

A pause. A silent question hovers between us, making the air thick to gulp down. *What's the difference between then and now?* The answer: *None.* Except now, the risks are higher. Now, the choices are between chancing the incantation and being burnt alive. I don't trust the odds, but I trust Mary.

I return my attention to my phone, remembering the series of photographs I took of my apartment after I finished unpacking and felt like an adult for the first time. I click on the camera roll and swipe until I find the pictures taken during my move-in date three years back. Before that, I shared the colonial style house on Chestnut Street, crashing on the couch except for the nights when my grandmother insisted I take her bed. Even in my early days of college, I squatted there instead of relocating to a dorm to save money. My grandmother never asked for rent. I repaid her with chauffeured trips to the grocery store and home-cooked meals on weeknights.

"This is where I need to go," I say, stretching the phone out to Mary. "Can you paint that?"

She dips her brush into the blood and paints, her eyes ping-ponging between the photograph and the canvas, copying every swivel and swoop. At times, the blood zigzags off course, but when it does, she wipes it with her sleeve. It stains the canvas, but she continues. We have to continue.

"This holds Polaroids?" she asks in the middle of tracing a window. "Do you have some of the two of us? When I'm older, I mean?"

"No. Yes. Well. I don't think we have time to look through them."

She looks at me a little too hard, a little too long. "I guess that's true."

To weave and dodge any further questions, I grab her backpack filled with ingredients. "I'll mix together the paste. I've done it before. At least I'll feel useful that way."

I hunt through my jean pockets, searching for a trace of my apartment to use as an ingredient, the same way I used the horseshoe for the farmhouse. I pull out a crumpled tissue, a faded receipt for birth control, and a key ring. A silver key dangles from the center, the only of its kind. I never handed a spare to an old boyfriend to *let himself in* or a neighbor to water the plants. My grandmother owned the only other copy. I made a duplicate for her at a department store with the Cancer logo, an outline of a crab, on the face. I kept the plain one for myself. With my key ready to work as a whisk, I move onto the next step. I scratch at my upper arm, fingernails digging into the original place where I cut myself open, until the wound seeps blood. I let it fall into the mixture, ground the herbs, squeeze the lemon, and mix it all with my room key.

While I work, my mind has the freedom to wander back to the first time I touched hemlock and jasmine, inside my apartment with sobs raising my chest. Even though my grandmother had reached the latter part of her life, even though I expected the Reaper to sink its claws into her sometime soon, actually having it happen rattled me. Stole a sliver of me.

But that was back when I considered her a saint. The one who rinsed my binky after I hurled it into the dirt. Who picked fresh oranges for my elementary-school friends to eat during soccer practice. Who rescued me up from a seedy bar at seventeen, no questions asked, even though I used a fake ID for entrance.

The truth complicates our relationship, taints the most beloved memories. I wonder whether tears will empty from my eyes at the funeral or whether anger will snatch them away. I might have to rewrite her eulogy. I might not want to give it in the first place.

"Everything has to be a problem," Mary says, launching me out of my daydreams.

"What's wrong?"

She stabs at the bottom of the jar with the pointed end of the brush. The thick red chunk cracks down the center. "The rest of this blood is too old. Dried out. I can't use this."

"Can we, I don't know, microwave it? Are microwaves invented?"

"We don't have one. And the kitchen is probably ash by now." Her lips squash to the side like an accordion. "But Rosie's room should be fine."

"Why would you go in there?"

She rises, dives out the door, and dashes down the hall without an explanation. The temptation to follow her is quickly squashed by my fear of charcoal skin.

When I watched horror movies behind my grandmother's back as a child (she shielded me from anything with violence), I thought of myself as a survivor. I compared myself to whoever made it to the end, dubbing myself a hero, a hotshot. Looking back, my grandmother wasn't the only person I was wrong about.

Mary returns coughing, her mouth hidden in the crook of her elbow. "Half the hallway is gone. I hope the fire didn't spread toward the barn, too. I hope the horses are okay."

"What did you get?"

She sits in front of her easel, but instead of lifting the brush, she lifts a blade and slashes her thigh, straight through the fabric.

"Jesus. What the fuck?" I ask, scrambling to make sense of the situation. For a second, I assume she has turned suicidal in an attempt to join her parents, to escape her sister.

Then she dips her brush into the open wound.

"I'm getting you back home," she says and uses the fresh blood as paint.

†

By the time the painting is half-finished, I have stuffed blankets beneath the door to prevent smoke from filling the room, but the heat touches me everywhere, dampening my forehead and wetting my armpits.

As for Mary, there are slits across both of her thighs, her stomach, and her non-dominant arm. Only a little blood ekes out each time, giving her one or two chances at most to re-wet the brush.

"This isn't working," she says, chucking her brush at the floor. "I need deeper cuts."

I intercept her hand as it reaches for the blade. "Let me do it this time. It's my turn."

"No. We've been using my blood since the beginning, since the jar. We're already taking a risk by not using actual paint. We at least have to stick to the same consistency. It has to be mine."

With her eyes pinched shut, she slides the metal against her wrist. It creates a deep wound. A hospital-worthy one. Blood erupts from the crack in her skin like a volcano, spilling over every edge, dying her skin scarlet.

I grope for a stray blanket to plug the wound, but she nudges me away before I can bandage her.

"This might be enough," she says, bending for her brush and returning to her work. She only stops to reposition the jar below her feet to catch any fallen drops.

The horror-movie version of me would steal her knife, force her to use my blood regardless of how it could impact the spell, and bleed while she healed.

In reality, my stomach heaves whenever her crisscross of cuts enters my sightline.

I stare out the window instead, resisting the urge to glance over at Mary as she dips, winces, and draws. Dips. Winces. Draws.

†

Five minutes pass. The fire crawls toward the doorway. The flames chew apart the wood. The smoke filters through the fresh openings, filling the room with a white haze.

The fumes corkscrew down my throat, clogging my lungs. I peel a sheet from the mattress and stuff it over my mouth, trying to calm my coughing.

When Mary motions for me to toss her another blanket, I assume she wants to smother the flames. Then I see her lean back, admire her illustration, and spiral the fabric around her wrist like gauze.

I swerve behind her, stealing a glance over her shoulder. "It looks perfect," I say, even though the thick lines make the final product look clumsy, clumpy. The canvas holds the shape of a generic building, but not the details of my specific apartment building. A good attempt under the circumstances, but shoddy compared to the original. I mutter a prayer inside my head. *Please be good enough. Please keep me safe.*

I dip my thumb into the concoction created earlier and form a triquetra on the picture, just like last time.

"I'm so sorry," I say before completing the final step. "I never should have come here."

"It's okay. It felt good to paint again. And it was a nice lie."

"What was?"

A rattling cough sputters from her cracked lips. "I know you're not my granddaughter."

The silence circles us like the flames, turning my cheeks amber. I wonder when she weeded out the truth. Not before arguing with her sister. Not before cutting herself open. No one, not even a saint, would sacrifice herself for a virtual stranger.

I open my mouth to form a reply, but I find it hard to lie. I find it even harder to tell the truth.

"It's impossible for me to be your grandmother," she continues, resting a hand on the back of mine. "If I was, I'd live through this."

I wobble my head. Squeeze her palm. "You could live through this."

"I don't regret helping you. I don't want you to feel bad. You didn't make me do this. Okay?"

The fire invades the room. Absorbs her door. Burns her rug. Gulps her headboard.

"Go home. Go to your real grandmother's funeral. Go say goodbye."

I watch mutely as the fire spreads further into the room, stealing every piece of furniture, every material memory. I am too much of a coward to risk a few minutes by carrying her out the window into the relative safety of the cornfields.

Instead, I turn away from the blood seeping from Mary's skin, the blanket darkening to red in her hands. With tears outlining my eyes, I speak the Latin phrase that sends me into the painting.

As my body bends, my bones crunch, and my skull collapses, I feel as evil as my grandmother.

CHAPTER XII

MARY

JANUARY 15, 2018

My eyes swung between the casket and the corkboard. Propped onto an easel, it held a cluster of photographs from the nineties and onward. Rosie bent over a baby crib while little hands nabbed at her pearls. Rosie dressed in an oversized, over-bright wizarding robe from the Halloween when her granddaughter went as a dragon. Rosie during that same granddaughter's graduation, handing her a bear dressed in a sweater that matched the school's colors.

In the last photo, Gillian looked the same as I recognized. Overlong hair. Dirty blonde. Curls clamped down with a straightener.

My mind shifted into reverse, snapping back eight decades. After Gillian had traveled through the painting, Rosie found me slashed and shredded, writhing in blood. She pulled me from the rubble of the building, risked her life shooting back inside to gather her spell book and materials, and smeared a fresh concoction across my wounds like paste. My gashes sewed themselves back together in time to save me, but eighty years later, the scars still stained my skin.

Every time I brushed my fingers across the bumps on my

stomach and wrists and thighs, they reminded me I'd saved a life—and that Rosie had saved mine. She never wanted me dead. She killed our parents to protect us. She kept me away from Felix because she thought he would hurt me the same way our father hurt her. She trapped me in that house to keep me from contacting the police because she heard stories of abusive foster parents and didn't want me transferred from one incestuous family to another.

It took three therapists to realize my sister's abuse had started at sixteen. When I'd asked her why she killed our parents, she had said, "Because you turn sixteen this week." The only explanation she'd ever made, the only clue she'd ever given, but it was enough to convince me to forgive her. For our parents. For the fire. All of it.

She deserved to hear my forgiveness, even if the Reaper had already stolen her voice, which is why I drove two hundred miles to find her.

"I'm sorry for your loss," I said to a middle-aged man at the head of the church, revealing missing teeth on either side of my front ones. "I know how much it hurts to lose a mother."

He enveloped my wrinkled hand in his. Shook it like glass. "Thank you for coming. How did you know her?"

After the farmhouse had erupted into ashes, Rosie found us new identities. New names. New IDs that claimed we were twenty-one. In a second attempt to save me, one that I mistook for hatred at the time, she made it so we weren't sisters anymore. She thought we were better off separated, so we never spoke again.

"We went to school together," I lied.

"Oh." He scratched inside his ear. "Ma never really talked about school. Or family. I figured her childhood wasn't the greatest."

"Sometimes it's best to keep your memories to yourself."

"Memories are all we have of her now, though."

"And pictures." I motioned toward the easel, filled with as much Gillian as Rosie. "Is her granddaughter here? I'd like to pay my respects."

"She usually always has her head in her phone, but she hasn't been answering her texts today. I think she's taking this harder than anybody else. They were best friends. Spent every Sunday together since she was a kid. Most weeks, more than that. I'm sure she'll show up soon, though. I can't imagine her missing her last chance at goodbye. And she's supposed to give the eulogy."

I nodded, chalking the coincidence up to fate. For decades, I had fought against the temptation to reach out to Gillian, especially once my husband (ten years younger and tech savvy) set up a Facebook account for me. I kept my distance to avoid muddying the waters. Left the past in the past to avoid complicating her future.

I checked up on Felix, though. I smiled wide at his profile picture, of him and a skinny blonde wife vacationing in Paris, sharing a kiss in front of the Eiffel Tower. The same place where my husband had proposed to me.

It took several months' worth of searching, but I even found Rosie's account, renamed Catherine Anne Hardwick. I had tracked her for years. A post on her page gave me the news about her passing. Someone posted the funeral dates and tagged her. Maybe the uncle who had spoken to me.

After changing into a tan suit, I'd gotten into my Oldsmobile with the radio off, practicing what to say to my sister in the dead silence. The questions I had pondered for years after the farmhouse burnt down no longer mattered. I had answered them on my own.

Why didn't you tell me what dad did? Because it was too horrible, too scarring, too embarrassing to say aloud. *Why did you kill mom, too?* Because she could have gone to the police. Because she could have found a resurrection incantation. Because, when it came down to it, she was complicit and deserved punishment as much as he did.

Inside the car, I failed to come up with a suitable speech, but after seeing Rosie with her curled blonde wig and olive dress, her ghost-pale skin and the cut slashed through her eyebrow, the words came easy. Like magic.

"I love you," I said, resting my knees on the velvet cushion in front of her coffin. "Thank you for saving my life. And thank you for turning yours around. You should be proud. You raised a great granddaughter. She's something you'll be able to brag about up there for a long time." I leaned down and fluttered a kiss against her forehead. "I'll see you soon, Rosie."

CHAPTER XIII

I am no longer in the farmhouse. I traveled through the painting. I felt my body shrink, extend, and dive through dimensions, but I am not inside of my empty bedroom. I am not inside of my apartment building.

The bloodied lines on the canvas must have been uneven. The picture must have come out inaccurately. The incantation failed to send me to my intended destination.

Instead of spilling tears at my grandmother's funeral, mourning her death and the death of the woman I thought I knew, I am alone in an ocean of red, swimming through blood as thick as quicksand. Every exhaled breath makes me feel like I am coughing up flames. My limbs ache. My stomach twists. My heart pounds like gunshots are firing inside my chest.

I am no longer in the farmhouse.

I am someplace much worse.

Holly Riordan is a full-time staff writer from Long Island, New York. She is the author of Lifeless Souls, a disturbing novella that details a future where technology becomes sentient. She has also published a creepy glow-in-the-dark poetry book called Severe(d). You can find her short science fiction and horror stories on Thought Catalog.

twitter.com/HollyyRio
www.instagram.com/hollyyrio
facebook.com/hollyriordanwriting
thoughtcatalog.com/holly-riordan

A digital
magazine
for thoughtful
storytelling.

THOUGHT CATALOG
www.thoughtcatalog.com

BROOKLYN, NY